A Note to Parents and Teachers

The *Dorling Kindersley Readers* series is a compelling reading program designed in conjunction with leading literacy experts, including Dr. Linda Gambrell, director of the School of Education at Clemson University. Dr. Gambrell has served on the board of directors of the International Reading Association and as president of the National Reading Conference.

The series combines a highly visual approach with engaging, easy-to-read text. Each reader is guaranteed to capture a child's interest while developing his or her reading skills, general knowledge, and love of reading.

The four levels of readers are aimed at different reading abilities, enabling you to choose the books that are exactly right for your children:

Level 1—Beginning to Read
Level 2—Beginning to Read Alone
Level 3—Reading Alone
Level 4—Proficient Readers

The "normal" age at which a child begins to read can be anywhere from three to eight years old, so these levels are intended only as a general guideline.

No matter which level you select, you can be sure that you are helping your child learn to read, then read to learn!

Dorling **DK** Kindersley

LONDON, NEW YORK, SYDNEY, DELHI, PARIS,
MUNICH, and JOHANNESBURG

Senior Editor Cynthia O'Neill
Editor Rebecca Knowles
Senior Managing Art Editor Cathy Tincknell
Publishing Manager Karen Dolan
Senior DTP Designer Andrew O'Brien
Production Nicola Torode
US Editor Gary Werner
Reading Consultant Linda Gambrell, PhD

First American Edition, 2000

00 01 02 03 04 05 10 9 8 7 6 5 4 3 2 1

Published in the United States by
Dorling Kindersley Publishing, Inc.
95 Madison Avenue
New York, New York 10016

**A catalog record for this book is available from
the Library of Congress.**

ISBN HC 0-7894-6675-9; PB 0-7894-6761-5

Printed and bound in the United States.

Illustrations by Paul Trevillion.
The publisher would like to thank the following for
their kind permission to reproduce their images:
Ronald Grant Archive: 44b.
Special photographers
Dave King, Andy Crawford and Richard Leeney

All other photographic images provided by World
Championship Wrestling, Inc.
Special thanks to Joseph Lester, WCW, Inc.

see our complete
catalog at
www.dk.com

Contents

DORLING KINDERSLEY *READERS*

GOING FOR
GOLDBERG

Written by Michael Teitelbaum

PROFICIENT
4
READERS

A Dorling Kindersley Book

Rising star

"Goldberg! Goldberg! Goldberg!"

The crowd chants his name. The mountain of muscles they call Goldberg is wrestling's greatest star. But where did his story begin? And how did he come to take World Championship Wrestling by storm?

William Scott Goldberg grew up in Tulsa, Oklahoma. He showed great athletic talent as a boy and was a star football player in high school. College scouts from all around the country came to watch him play.

Goldberg accepted a college scholarship to the University of Georgia. He played for their football team, the Georgia Bulldogs, and became captain of the defensive team. As a defensive lineman, he won awards for game-saving plays, hustle on the field, and tackles.

He also studied hard, and earned a degree in psychology.

Fearless
As teenagers, Goldberg and his two brothers loved to fly gliders and acrobatic planes. This, along with his football training, helped build his "no fear" attitude.

Football player
During college, Goldberg was a member of the "Junkyard Dog Club." Only the football team's best defensive players could join this select club!

Teams
As a pro, Goldberg was first drafted by the Los Angeles Rams, and then went on to play for the Atlanta Falcons.

After college, Goldberg became a professional football player. He played in the National Football League (NFL) until 1994, when injuries forced him to retire.

What would this powerful athlete do next?

Goldberg was a formidable sight on the football field

Panthers
After his career with the Falcons ended, Goldberg was picked up by the newly formed Carolina Panthers in 1995. Injuries kept him from ever playing with the team.

Goldberg was introduced to the world of professional wrestling through a series of chance meetings. His brother Mike shared a house with the wrestler Ric Flair. Then, while working out in the gym, Goldberg became friends with the wrestlers Sting and Lex Luger. They encouraged him to try his hand at wrestling. Finally, while out to dinner one night in Atlanta, Goldberg met Diamond Dallas Page (DDP).

"I took one look at Goldberg and told him, 'you need to be with us in WCW'," Page says.

Fortunately for wrestling fans, Goldberg followed DDP's advice.

Before *we* follow Goldberg's rise to the top of WCW, let's look at the special style and unique moves that have made Goldberg such a great champion.

DDP
Diamond Dallas Page actually started in wrestling as a manager, developing the talents of others. He made his own debut as a wrestler in 1991 and became one of the great stars of WCW.

Jimmy Hart
Goldberg's
theme was
produced by
Jimmy Hart.
As well as
being a famous
wrestling
manager,
Hart is a rock
musician.
He used to
play in a rock
band called
the Gentrys.

Explosive entrance

His theme music blasts from the
speakers in the arena. The crowd rises
to its feet and cheers. They know
Goldberg is about to make his
entrance. And what an entrance it is!

It begins when Doug Dellinger, WCW's head of security, knocks on the locker room door. Beside him stand two security guards.

The door bursts open and Goldberg marches toward the ring. The security guards walk on either side of him—to protect everyone else from the most dangerous man in championship wrestling!

As Goldberg enters the arena, fireworks explode from the floor. He is bathed in sparks and smoke. As the fireworks end, Goldberg blows out a stream of smoke.

He charges into the ring, throwing punches in the air while the sound of explosions fills the arena. The crowd knows he's ready for action as he bellows his trademark phrase: "Who's next?!"

Special events
WCW stages 12 pay-per-view spectaculars each year, such as Souled Out, which takes place every February.

Muscle mountain
Goldberg is 6'3" and weighs 285 pounds.

Signature moves

Goldberg's style inside the ring can be defined by one word: aggressive! He's even been known to take on two opponents at a time.

But he is most famous for his signature finishing moves: the Spear and the Jackhammer. When the champ unleashes these moves, no one is left standing...except the crowd, up on its feet and cheering!

Family ties
How does Goldberg's family feel when they see him in action, ready to flatten an opponent? He says that at first they were dismayed by his decision to be a wrestler, but now they are his biggest fans.

Goldberg flattens Sting with the Spear

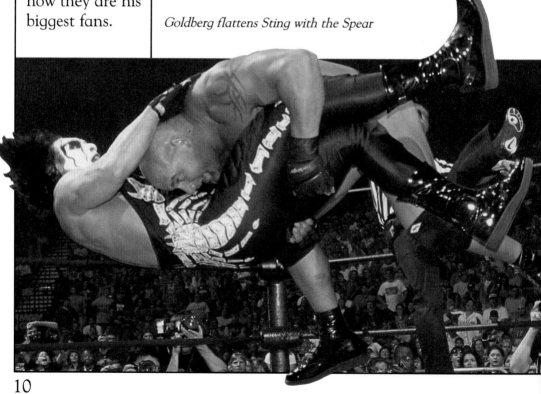

The Spear is taken from the days when Goldberg played football as a defensive linesman. He launches himself into a football tackle, aimed right at his opponent's mid-section. His opponent lands on the mat with a crunch.

Now Goldberg is ready to perform the Jackhammer. This is a devastating finishing move and usually it ends the match.

First, Goldberg lifts his opponent into the air and carries him around the ring. Then he leaps up and slams his victim to the mat.

Finally, Goldberg turns his body and lands on his opponent with 285 pounds of muscle.

Match over!

Goldberg wins!

Goldberg slams Ernest Miller with a Jackhammer.

The ring
The average WCW wrestling "ring" is in fact a square, which measures about 18 feet across! They weigh almost 6,000 pounds.

WCW debut

The Goldberg phenomenon began on September 22, 1997. That was when Goldberg made his first TV appearance on Monday Nitro, WCW's Monday-night wrestling program.

Power Plant
Each month, about 15 people take part in a three-day tryout to become WCW wrestlers. Up to three people are accepted for the six-month training program at the Power Plant.

Goldberg had spent the previous months at the Power Plant, the training center where would-be wrestlers prepare to enter the action-packed world of the WCW. Now, after intensive training, Goldberg was ready to make his debut.

His opponent was the veteran wrestler Hugh Morrus. For all his experience, Morrus was completely unprepared for the powerhouse he was about to face.

Goldberg climbed into the ring. He stared coldly at Morrus as the bell rang to begin the match.

As Goldberg begins a fight, every bit of his concentration is focused on the job at hand.

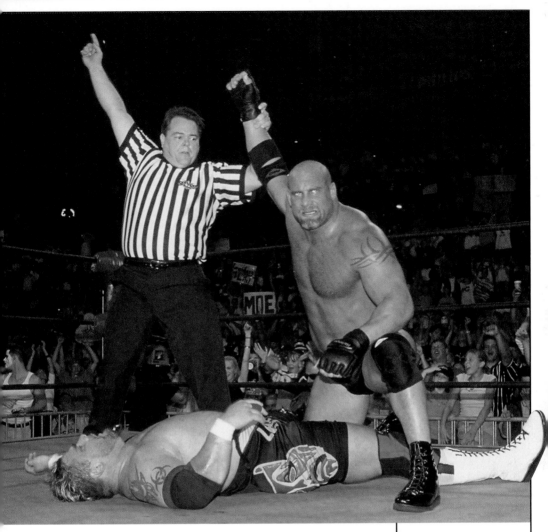

Morrus wonders what went wrong, as Goldberg is declared the winner.

It only took a couple of minutes for Goldberg to get the upper hand. Moments later, the match was over. Goldberg had demolished Morrus.

Victory number one was already under his belt.

Hugh Morrus
Morrus is all animal in the ring! He's known for his hyena-like laugh and his battle technique, which has been compared to a charging rhino.

First championship

After this first triumph, Goldberg continued to win match after match. He beat his opponents with ease because his determination, strength, and devastating finishing moves were too much for them.

Soon, Goldberg was meeting mid-ranked wrestlers. He powered his way through them, as well.

It was around this time that Goldberg had a run-in with the rebel wrestlers known as the nWo. The nWo had realized that Goldberg was on his way to the top—and so the bad boys of wrestling thought it was time to intimidate him. Before he had ever battled an nWo member in a WCW match, Goldberg was attacked outside the ring by a swarm of nWo thugs.

It didn't stop him. Goldberg continued to wow the WCW fans.

During one amazing spell, from
March 26 to March 30, 1998,
he fought veteran wrestler Jerry
Flynn every night, in five different
arenas. Goldberg demolished
Flynn every time!

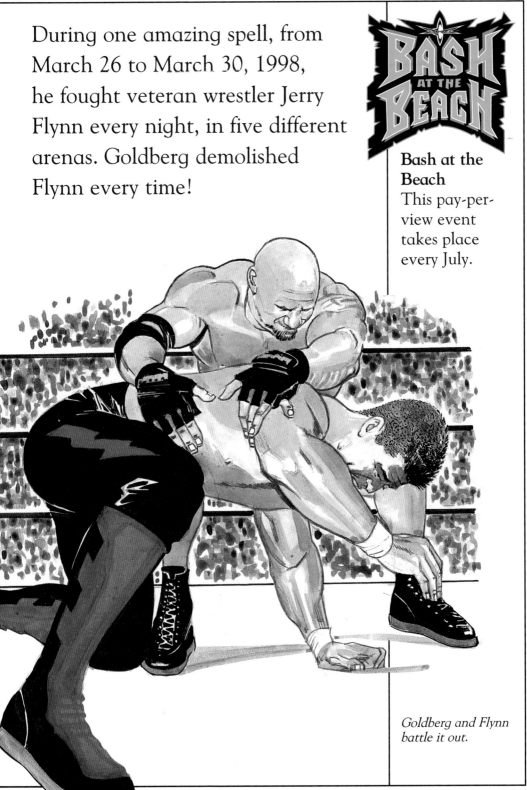

Bash at the Beach
This pay-per-view event takes place every July.

Goldberg and Flynn battle it out.

Belt of pride
When a wrestler wins a championship, the WCW presents him with a belt. The belt is rumored to be made of solid gold, with leather straps, and is said to weigh a hefty ten pounds.

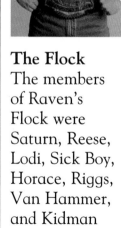

The Flock
The members of Raven's Flock were Saturn, Reese, Lodi, Sick Boy, Horace, Riggs, Van Hammer, and Kidman (*above*).

During Spring Stampede 1998, Goldberg had a major victory over a wrestler called Saturn. Saturn took the defeat badly. This was the start of a long-running feud between the two men.

On April 20, 1998, Goldberg took on the wrestler named Raven for the WCW US Championship. At the time, Raven was leader of a group of wrestlers called the Flock.

It was an exciting, close-fought match. The advantage flipped back and forth and it was impossible to say who would win.

At one point, when things were going well for Goldberg, other members of the Flock jumped into the ring to help Raven. Goldberg defeated each one.

Finally, Goldberg finished Raven off with the Jackhammer.

The fight was over. Goldberg was the new US champion.

Many Champions
There are five different categories of championship in WCW: World, US, Tag team, Hardcore, and Cruiserweight.

La Parka
During May and June 1998, Goldberg won 16 matches, including a victory over La Parka, a Mexican wrestler whose name means "the Mask."

World champion

Goldberg's feud with Saturn continued after the new champion had won his first belt. In May and June 1998, Goldberg fought and defeated Saturn ten times!

Goldberg also proved himself to be a loyal friend in this time. During one Monday Nitro, his friend Kevin Greene was attacked by fellow wrestlers the Giant and Curt Hennig.

At the time, Greene wasn't even in the ring; he was giving an interview!

Later that night, while Greene wrestled the Giant, Hennig jumped into the ring. He unfairly helped the Giant attack Greene.

Goldberg rushed to the rescue. He jumped into the ring, quickly disposing of the Giant and Hennig.

Throughout the spring and early summer of 1998, Goldberg tore through WCW like a tornado. Finally, it was announced that the young challenger would face Hulk Hogan (then known as Hollywood Hogan) for the WCW World Championship.

Curt Hennig Hennig made his debut in 1979. He has been a major wrestling star ever since.

With every victory, Goldberg made more and more fans.

Hogan's Legdrop
Hulk Hogan's legdrop begins when his opponent is already lying on the mat. First Hulk runs off the ropes. Then he jumps up and drops a leg over his rival's face and neck, pinning him to the mat.

Victory roar
When Goldberg wins a match, he often turns to the crowd and gives a mighty roar of triumph.

On July 6, 1998, Goldberg was ready to take on Hogan. But first, he had a nasty surprise. Before he could wrestle the champ, Goldberg was made to fight Scott Hall, one of Hogan's nWo buddies. It was a tough match, but Goldberg won.

Finally, Goldberg met Hogan. At first, Hogan dominated the fight. He hit Goldberg with two legdrops, but he couldn't pin the challenger.

Goldberg kicked out of the legdrops. He nailed Hogan with a Spear, and followed with the Jackhammer for "the pin."

Hogan was beaten. The WCW had a new world champion!

Monday Nitro Many of Goldberg's greatest matches have appeared on Monday Nitro, the popular WCW program which first appeared in 1995.

Music fan
You might be surprised to learn that Goldberg is a country music fan. One of his favorite groups is the Charlie Daniels Band.

FALL BRAWL

Fall Brawl
At Fall Brawl 98 DDP tried to flee his clash with Goldberg. The champ stopped him!

Who's next?

Goldberg started winning WCW matches in 1997. Little did anyone know then that this would be the start of the longest winning streak in wrestling history. Eventually, Goldberg won 175 fights in a row.

As WCW World Champion, Goldberg had to take on all challengers and watch out for the nWo, too. Hogan's nWo buddies were looking for revenge after Hogan's defeat.

Once, as Goldberg was busy in the arena trashing Brian Adams, the nWo were busy trashing Goldberg's dressing room! The champ didn't let such tactics affect his focus.

He concentrated on beating everyone in sight.

Next, the nWo ganged up on Goldberg's friend DDP during a match. Goldberg tried to come to the rescue, but the Giant prevented him.

Goldberg now had it out for the Giant. He wanted to beat him.

Brian Adams
Adams joined WCW in 1998, teaming up with the nWo right away. His tag team partners have included Curt Hennig and Sting.

Scott Hall
A co-founder of the nWo, Hall has been a constant thorn in Goldberg's side. Their clashes have been among the most exciting, and controversial, in WCW.

Battle Royale
In this type of match, up to 24 wrestlers fight in the ring at the same time. The last man standing is the winner!

At the Battle Royale in the summer of 1998, Goldberg had to face six wrestlers before he got his shot at the Giant. And that's what he did! Goldberg eliminated Scott Hall, Konnan, Curt Hennig, Scott Norton, Sting, *and* Lex Luger before he faced the Giant.

Goldberg took everything the Giant threw at him. He nailed the Giant with a Spear, then pinned him with a Jackhammer for the victory.

Hogan emphasized that he wanted to battle Goldberg by slamming the champ with a chair!

During this time, Hogan made it clear that he wanted to fight with Goldberg again. At a Monday Nitro, Hogan nailed the champ with a chair. Kevin Nash, an nWo founder, yanked the chair away from Hogan. When Goldberg spotted Nash with the chair, he speared Nash, mistakenly thinking that Nash had hit him.

Goldberg had made a new enemy.

Skin's Match
WCW has seen wrestlers clash over unusual prizes—such as the "skin's match" where Tank Abbott battled with Big Al over Al's beloved leather jacket.

Goldberg simply would not be intimidated by Hogan...or anyone else!

25

Causing havoc
Goldberg first caught the eye of WCW fans at Halloween Havoc 1997, when he leapt into the ring and floored Steve McMichael.

Weeks later, the incident seemed forgotten. Goldberg and Nash paired up in a tag team match against Hogan and the Giant. But during the battle, Nash jumped into the ring to help Goldberg and ended up smashing him with his boot.

Was it an accident—or had Nash planned it? Tensions between Nash and Goldberg built further.

At Halloween Havoc that year, Goldberg fought his great friend, Diamond Dallas Page (*below*).

It was an epic battle. At first
DDP trapped Goldberg in his famous
Diamond Cutter; but with typical
strength and skill, the champion
broke free. Goldberg finally won,
using the Jackhammer.

There were no bad feelings
after the match. The close
friends embraced in the spirit
of sportsmanship that has
always been the basis of
Goldberg's career.

But as fall changed to
winter in late 1998, a wrestler
who cared little about
sportsmanship prepared
to end wrestling's greatest
winning streak.

That wrestler was
Kevin Nash.

*Goldberg and DDP may be
friends—but that doesn't stop
DDP from trying any tactic to
win their fights!*

Anything goes
In a no disqualification match, no holds are barred. No one can be disqualified for breaking the rules. The match is over when one of the wrestlers is unable to continue.

Losing
Goldberg thinks that the fight where he lost the championship was the strangest match he ever took part in. "What made it even stranger was that it happened on my birthday!" he says.

The streak ends

On December 27, 1998, Goldberg clashed with Kevin Nash in a "no disqualification" match. The World Heavyweight Championship was on the line. So was Goldberg's streak of 175 straight victories.

Goldberg fought bravely, even though at one stage he was battling Nash, Disco Inferno, and Bam Bam Bigelow all at once.

Then Scott Hall entered the ring and hit Goldberg—with a stun gun. Goldberg collapsed to the mat. On a normal night, the challenger would have been disqualified for using a weapon. But not this night.

Goldberg had lost. Nash was the world champion.

Starrcade
Goldberg's incredible streak of victories finally came to an end during Starrcade 1998. The Starrcade event, which takes place in December, has been around since 1983. Goldberg has had other memorable Starrcades, including 1999 when he fought an epic battle with Bret Hart.

Kevin Nash jumps back just in time, as Goldberg lashes out.

The Rematch

In January 1999, Goldberg faced Nash in another "no disqualification" match. It was his attempt to regain the world title. But again, events were overtaken by an nWo plot.

Before the match began, the police arrested Goldberg. The nWo had laid false harrassment charges against him! When Goldberg finally returned to the arena, he was furious.

He found Hogan, Hall, and other nWo members in the ring celebrating his arrest. The former champ burst into the ring and pounded one foe after another.

But then Scott Hall brought out his stun gun. He knocked Goldberg out and painted "nWo" on his body.

Since then, Goldberg has fought to regain the world title many times.

Charges
Goldberg was arrested and charged with harrassing a woman. A live TV Nitro audience saw the police lead Goldberg away in handcuffs. Throughout the program, the audience saw Goldberg being held at the police station, until he finally proved the charges were false and returned to the ring.

He has not succeeded, although he regained the WCW US title in October 1999.

But being a winner is not just about titles. For his many fans, his decency, power, and spirit mean that Goldberg will always be a champion of champions.

Sid Vicious

Goldberg vs the bad guys
Asked if there was anything he would change about WCW, Goldberg speaks his mind: "If I could change one thing, it would be to kick out all the bad guys, so that we'd have nothing but fun, and present a positive image to kids."

Goldberg broke free of Sid Vicious' choke hold to regain the WCW US Championship title.

Lex Luger
Luger has won the WCW World Championship twice, as well as other titles.

Greatest foes

Goldberg has been wrestling for only a few years, but he has faced all the stars of the sport. Meet the rivals that he has wrestled on his way to the top.

Kevin Nash

At 6'11" and 329 pounds, and with a signature maneuver known as the Jack Knife Power Bomb, Kevin Nash is a wrestler to take very seriously!

He has always been an outsider, and was a major member of the nWo, the rebel group that challenged WCW.

A high point in his career was ending Goldberg's winning streak.

Kevin Nash has won the WCW World Heavyweight Championship title three times.

Scott Hall

Scott Hall is wrestling's hottest bad boy. He cofounded the nWo (New World Order), the rebel group that tried to overturn WCW. He considers himself an outlaw. And at 6'5" and 280 pounds, no one is going to argue with him!

Hall has been a professional wrestler since 1984, but his biggest impact has been within WCW. He fought and lost to Goldberg a number of times during Goldberg's winning streak. He then helped bring the streak to an end, when he brought a stun gun into the wrestling ring.

Billy Kidman
Kidman is one of the best athletes in pro wrestling. He combines a high-flying aerial style with classic mat moves.

Scott Steiner
The wrestler known as Big Poppa Pump was an NCAA wrestling champ. Steiner caused nothing but trouble for Goldberg and WCW when he joined up with the nWo.

Legendary
When people think of wrestling, they think of Hulk Hogan. No one believed that Goldberg could defeat him.

Hulk Hogan

He's the most famous wrestler of all time. He's also a movie star, a former presidential candidate, and the voice behind a famous cartoon character! Is there anything Hulk Hogan can't do? Since joining WCW in June 1994, he has earned eight world championships titles. When he changed his name to "Hollywood Hogan," he adopted a mean identity and cofounded the nWo. He's now back to being the Hulkster, one of wrestling's all-time greats.

Diamond Dallas Page

This powerful wrestler finishes off his opponents with the Diamond Cutter, one of the most devastating finishing moves in wrestling. Yet, despite his fearsome power, Page is a likable "people's champion." He has been a tag team partner to celebrities like the NBA's Karl Malone and TV's Jay Leno.

Page, who is known as DDP, is a former wrestling manager and didn't start wrestling until he was in his 30s! He and Goldberg are two of WCW's "good guys." They are close friends, although their matches against each other have provided some of wrestling's greatest thrills.

Buff Bagwell
Buff (*below*) has won three WCW World Tag Team titles, with three different partners.

Bam Bam Bigelow
Forget the cute name—Bam Bam is really scary! His huge head is covered with tattoos, adding to his overall air of menace.

Bret Hart

Bret "Hitman" Hart is the most famous Canadian wrestler in history. His father, Stu, was also a pro wrestler. He obviously trained his son well, for Bret has held the World Heavyweight Title seven times. His skill and toughness make the Hitman one powerful force.

Hart has wrestled with Goldberg as a tag team partner, but he has also defeated the former champ during Goldberg's attempts to regain his world title.

When he's not winning matches, Hart is a columnist and cartoonist for the *Calgary Sun* newspaper.

Hart's finishing move, the Sharpshooter

Sid Vicious

This ruthless bundle of raw power has torn through the world of wrestling. Finishing off opponents with the Power Bomb, his finishing move, Sid became US and world champion. He put together a winning streak of over 150 matches, second only to Goldberg's. In fact, Goldberg ended Sid's winning streak.

When he's not wrestling, Sid loves to play softball. He even has a batting cage and pitching machine in his back yard.

Meng
Meng is expertly trained in nine forms of martial arts. His expertise and serious attitude make him a force to be reckoned with in WCW.

Toughest fights

Goldberg has fought some epic battles on his way to the top. His struggles against the nWo were some of the most exciting matches in WCW history. His clashes against Nash and Hogan have brought WCW fans to the edge of their seats.

Recently, Goldberg was asked to pick his *all-time* toughest opponent. He chose Paul Wight—the Giant.

nWo havoc
Whenever one member of the nWo was in the ring, others were sure to follow. Kevin Nash (*below left*) sometimes stood by and watched as his teammates, like Scott Hall (*right*), did their dirty work.

When the Giant fought in WCW, he stood 7ft tall and weighed over 500 pounds. He and Goldberg did battle many times.

Since the Jackhammer involves Goldberg lifting an opponent up over his head, the champ wondered if he could even pick the Giant up. He did, again and again, beating the Giant each time in titanic battles.

Lumberjack match
In this match, wrestlers stand outside the edge of the ring and throw back wrestlers trying to escape it!

Own name
Many wrestlers take on bizarre nicknames, but Goldberg isn't one of them. "I decided to use my real name when I wrestled, so I could always be myself," he says.

Food for life
A good diet is an important part of Goldberg's fitness routine. "I stay away from fatty foods and keep to a high protein, low-carbohydrate diet," he says.

The right stuff
Wanna-be WCW heavyweight wrestlers must be aged between 18 to 28 and stand at least 5'9" tall. Most weigh more than 180 pounds.

Fitness routine

A muscular body like Goldberg's doesn't develop by accident.

His sculpted physique is the result of hard work, commitment, and hundreds of hours in the gym. To develop and maintain his body, Goldberg follows a regular routine.

"I work out four or five days a week, for about an hour a day," Goldberg explains. "Two or three days a week, I do cardio kickboxing. Cardio work is very important. It strengthens the heart and increases lung capacity, and keeps me from getting out of breath during a match."

But that's just the beginning.

"Four or five days a week I do a regular routine of weight training to keep my muscles strong," Goldberg continues. "Every other day, I concentrate on working my neck muscles to strengthen the Spear.

The rest of my fitness routine takes place in the ring. You might call it 'on-the-job' training."

Goldberg at work in the gym.

Goldberg is a role model to many young people, and he takes this responsibility seriously. "Don't let anybody ever tell you that you don't have the ability to do something," he says. "Don't sell yourself short. Always remember who you are and where you come from."

Weightlifting
Bodybuilders
use free weights
like these to
define and
shape their
bodies.

Goldberg's hard work
in the gym was never more
important than when he injured
a ligament in his knee during
Slamboree, in May 1999. After
surgery, he began the hard work of
getting his left leg back into shape.

A lot of the work focused on
balance and stability. Strengthening
the muscles around the ligament
was vital to Goldberg's recovery, too.

Next came full-force kicks to
heavy bags, the kind that boxers
practice with. This helped build up
power in Goldberg's leg.

As his knee improved,
Goldberg wasn't happy
with just returning to the
fitness level he had before
the injury. He wanted
to go even further.
He worked on a few new
moves, including one
called the Chainsaw.

Dedication
Goldberg's former personal trainer, Timothy Catalfo, says, "Every single day, Bill Goldberg trains with the intensity of an 18-year-old trying to earn a scholarship for school. I've never seen someone fight so hard to improve himself."

Monster spirit
Catalfo himself is a former wrestler. Japanese fans gave him the nickname "Obake," meaning "spirit" and "monster," when he defeated 17 opponents in less than 35 minutes!

All the hard work paid off. On Monday Nitro in July 1999, Goldberg returned to the ring. When the fireworks and smoke of his trademark entrance cleared, there stood Goldberg, the very picture of physical conditioning.

Goldberg in action in Universal Soldier, The Return.

On screen

Out of the arena, Goldberg has been featured on a number of TV shows, including *The Tonight Show with Jay Leno, Live with Regis and Kathie Lee,* and *The Dennis Miller Show.*

He made his TV acting debut on *The Love Boat,* alongside Kevin Nash. They played tag team partners. The storyline centered around Goldberg getting married.

After Goldberg got a taste of acting, he wanted more. His first movie project was *Universal Soldier, The Return*. On that film, he worked with Jean Claude Van Damme and played a character named Romeo.

His next project was a made-for-TV movie, *The Jesse Ventura Story*.

Most recently, he starred in the WCW and Warner Brothers' wrestling-based comedy, *Ready To Rumble*. Goldberg played a familiar role—one of the world's greatest wrestlers!

"I was always very curious about what it would be like to be in a movie," Goldberg says. "It was a great experience. I hope there are many more in the future."

Goldberg says he would love to become a movie actor when he retires from wrestling.

Ready to rumble
This comedy features many WCW stars. Most play themselves, but Kanyon (*above*) acted as stunt double for one of the lead actors, Oliver Platt. Super-fit Kanyon had to wear body padding to look more like the plump actor.

Helping out
Goldberg feels that his success and fame have given him something far more precious than money—the ability to help young people. "That's what I cherish more than anything else that I get from wrestling," he says. "It's an honor to be able to do what I do. It really is."

Big guy, big heart

Goldberg loves kids. "The best part of being Goldberg," he once said, "is being able to make a difference in a kid's life."

He has certainly done that. When he's not in the ring, you can usually find Goldberg helping out children's charities, like the Make-A-Wish Foundation. This organization grants the wishes of children who are very ill. Often, that wish is to meet a real-life superhero like Goldberg. He never lets them down.

He also helps raise money for the Starlight Foundation, which works for terminally ill children. Goldberg recently took part in an event that helped raise six million dollars to build a new building for this charity.

In addition, Goldberg is a spokesman for the Humane Society, and speaks out for animal rights.

He tries to increase awareness on this issue and has even spoken about it to the US Congress.

No doubt about it, Goldberg is a true champion—both in and out of the ring!

Animal rights
Goldberg uses his popularity to get across the message of the Humane Society. The organization was founded in 1954 and exists to help protect all animals.

Glossary

Acrobatic
Daring and graceful, showing great skill and agility.

Advantage
A better position than someone else.

Aerial
In the air.

Attitude
The way a person views a situation.

Cardio
Related to strengthening the heart.

Columnist
A person who writes a regular feature for newspapers or magazines.

Confrontation
Facing someone with hostile intent.

Cunning
Clever or sly, someone who plans and plots.

Debut
The first time someone does something or something happens.

Defensive Lineman
Football position. A defensive player who plays at the line of scrimmage (where the ball is placed before a play begins).

Dispose
Get rid of.

Disqualified
Declared the loser for breaking the laws or rules of the game.

Drafted
To be chosen by a team.

Embrace
Hug.

Encourage
To push someone, in a positive way, to do something.

Feud
Quarrel or dispute.

Finishing move
The standard moves that a wrestler uses to win a match.

Formidable
Hard to overcome, inspiring fear or dread

Glider
A small plane, with no engine, that rides the wind currents.

Martial arts
Self-defense techniques.

Opponent
A rival; someone who belongs to the opposite team.

Phenomenon
Remarkable person, event, or thing.

Pin
In wrestling, to hold an opponent's shoulders to the mat for a count of three. This results in winning the match.

Psychology
The study of the mind and how it works.

Renegade
Someone who rejects rules and behaves poorly.

Ruthless
Not caring about anyone else. Mean and cruel.

Scout
A person representing a team, who watches an athlete and judges their ability to see if that athlete is right for his or her team.

Stable
Firmly in place.

Stun gun
A weapon used by police officers. It gives out an electric shock that knocks out its victim.

Tag team
Usually, a team of two wrestlers. During a tag-team match, wrestlers from each team take turns wrestling or resting.